The 'Issue' of Flappity Maya

E. Adonz.

29/07/2023

Commendations for *The 'Issue' of Flappity Maya*

"As a Year 5 teacher I would love to share these enchanting stories with my own class. The children of the fictional Goldilocks class seem to need some of the excellent emotional, social and moral pointers provided by the story of Margarine Cops. The barriers faced by the protagonist are all well within the experience of contemporary children; while the author writes with the knowledge and experience of an accomplished KS2 leader. This is an engaging book and one filled with examples to promote story telling and discussion."

Mr. David Boyer
Year 5 Teacher
Buckinghamshire, UK

"Full of wit and so much depth! Though fictional, this book captures the intricacies of the mind as it journeys into the crucial quest of who we are. It creatively unveils the different ways trauma can show up and the different shapes it can take. Though at times upsetting, the resilience of Margarine is cause for celebration."

Dr. Precious Koce
Clinical Psychologist
Essex, UK

The 'Issue' of Flappity Maya

Elizabeth Ngozi Adonu

The Smart Reading Child Project
www.smartreadingchild.com

ISBN-13: 979-8853482029

ISBN-10: 8853482029

Educators and libraries, for a variety of smart reading children ideas, visit:

The Smart Reading Child Project
www.smartreadingchild.com

CONTENTS

DEDICATION

To the spirit of any young people who are striving to develop their potential through enthusiastic reading.

ACKNOWLEDGMENTS

Certain wonderful individuals deserve my appreciation and gratitude:

Dr. Joseph Adonu (my husband and No.1 fan!) whose intellectual passion and design prowess guided me to complete and publish this current and previous books as part of the Smart Reading Child Project.

To Zanetor, my daughter, for her meticulous creation of the necessary illustrations for the book, and for her patience in listening to my ideas, reading through my drafts and freely giving me her honest and priceless opinion.

To Dexter, my son, for his support from afar.

Also, to all my friends, colleagues, family and everyone who has provided some support and inspiration towards completing this book.

Finally, *Soli Deo Gloria.*

FLAPPITY POEMS

The Champion Skater

i.
Tile- Glider
Arm-Twirler
Chin- Lifter
Body- Prancer.

ii.
Rhythm - Creator
Leg -Twister
Mood - Enhancer
Joy – Stimulator.

iii.
Laughter - Evoker
Audience –Enchanter
Crowd -Gatherer
Environment – Changer

Question:

Can you decode the message in this poem?

What type of poem is this?

Grass To Grace

i.

Rising from grass
She had not a pass
Her life, long waned
Her mind like a plane.

ii.

Then the tick
Before the click
She had a peek
The glow on her cheek.

iii

Behold
She was bold
Her mind no longer torn
A Champion was soon born.

Question:

Can you decode the message in this poem?

What type of poem is this?

v

Goldilocks Class

It was a warm and beautiful summer afternoon. The sun was strikingly golden and the sky was thinly layered with pillows of cloud. The whispers of breeze made a classroom a rather unappealing place to be. All the children in Year 6 Goldilocks Class of Springdale Montgomery School, sat in their seats chatting noisily as they waited for the register but with looks of disinterest in any form of classroom learning or engagement for the afternoon. "Hey Luke!" shouted Ralph. "What is a mammal?" Luke turned shyly to the loud-mouthed Ralph and whispered, "it's a fruit spread. My mum makes it all the time." "Hahahaha!" cackled Ralph, "silly Billy, it's not a fruit spread, that would be marmalade! A mammal is a person who is stupid!" he further retorted. "Hahahaha," the whole class broke into laughter. "No, Ralph," whispered Luke undeterred, "a stupid person is called a moron, and that would be you!" he calmly added, sending the class into yet another raucous laughter. "Okay, another question," Ralph continued, invigorated by the laughter, unperturbed by his own porous knowledge and completely unaware that his intelligence had just been dealt a blow by Luke. Ralph was the typical class clown who often mistook being laughed at for being laughed with.

So, undeterred, he ranted on; "hey Luke, what do you call an animal which walks on four limbs, has a tail and barks a lot?" With a mischievous spread on his face, Luke opened his mouth and yelped, "it's called W...RR..WRALPH WRALPH!" The whole class collapsed with hilarity. "Enough, children, the circus isn't here yet!" Mrs. Nibbs the class teacher interrupted in a slightly raised voice. Ralph growled, as usual, not ready to stop the comedy. "Right, Ralph Wallace Wolfe, I said stop it or you'll growl and bark for the rest of the afternoon!" Mrs. Nibbs added in a sterner tone. She danced her way over to a bookshelf and picked up a Mathematics textbook with 2 written on it to indicate key stage 2, in preparation for the afternoon's lesson.

Theo Fellus, the class nose picker, sat in a chair by himself. He did not look happy. "Please Miss," he begged, as Mrs. Nibbs walked past his table. Mrs. Nibbs pretended she didn't hear. She had a busy afternoon to contend with and was not about to listen to one of Theo's never-ending stories. "Miss, Miss, Miss?" Theo continued, almost chiming like a neglected and demented cuckoo clock. There was still no response. "Mrs. Nibbs!" Theo screamed with persistence. Mrs. Nibbs dropped the textbook in alarm, firing a frown at Theo, who at this time was wearing a look as innocent as a baby. "Theo Fellus, that is not a classroom voice!" Mrs. Nibbs *chided. "I will not have you turning this place into a market!" she continued. "Not a market Miss, you usually say post office," Theo proceeded to correct Mrs. Nibbs. "Okay Miss," he added, "but would you please read us a story?" he asked very harmlessly and followed to pick the insides of his nose. With a look of dismay, Mrs. Nibbs quickly reached for a tissue and handed it to Theo to stop him from eating every clog of phlegm hanging out his nostrils. "Story! Story! Story!" the whole class chanted in unison. Mrs. Nibbs found herself cornered so she obliged, putting away the Maths textbook for another day. "Alright, alright!" she conformed. "As it's sunny and warm, I think we should make it an outdoor learning. Maybe we could use the forest school grass corner," she suggested with a smile. "Right, come on then, let's go out for an afternoon story." Mrs. Nibbs completed the register, picked a storybook off her special bookshelf, and made her way to the door. The children followed her, full of buzz and chatting with excitement. "There's nothing more appealing than an afternoon of story reading," whispered Meggie to Narissa. "Especially if the reader is the phenomenally melodious Mrs. Nibbs," Phoebe contributed.*

Everyone sat on the immaculately mowed green grass, enthusiasm written all over their faces. Mrs.

Nibbs cleared her throat and selected her most musical story reading voice. She closed her eyes, took a deep breath wearing a broad smile. "Once upon a time," her enchanting voice started. Mrs. Nibbs read the story of 'The 'Issue' of Flappity Maya," a one-time notoriously unruly child who learnt to tame her energies and became a champion skater.

This is the story Mrs. Nibbs read to the children………

1

Doomed before her birth

Once upon a time, in years far gone, in a kingdom of monarchs, laid the 'Land of the Angles', England as it's currently called. The Land of the Angles was a country where oceans rose to meet mountains and skies were scraped by buildings. With fluffy clouds and perpetual rainbows, the Land of the Angles was an enigma; an island the size of an elephant's palm yet thriving with so much intensity, giants met to party on her corridors. There, hidden in a suburban enclave, was a skater, a girl with magical limbs. She was a prancer, a twirler and mood changer; spectacular and amazing to watch. She was able to enchant merely with the patter of her feet and the turnings of her shoes. Her feet, trim and delicate in her tiny skating shoes could slide from here to there, yet she had the most ridiculous name - Margarine Cops! Margarine Cops was slightly different from your average girl. Even her name came with a burst.

As an adolescent, Margarine won countless local skating trophies as well as three major regional trophies. At the age of 15 she was on her way to winning the prestigious national skating title, an achievement that had been beyond her wildest dreams.

You see, as a child, Margarine hadn't always been successful, happy or popular. She didn't think she could do anything good, so she didn't make the effort. She was a 'different' child, with extraordinary problems; the kind of child who often said the wrong thing, even with the best of intentions. Yes, Margarine typified the awkward child, often without a friend and the kind who hated her names. "Margarine Cops? For goodness sakes, who are my parents then? Bread and Coffee? Or maybe I must have descended from generations of police officers!" Margarine often spewed out to anyone who cared to listen. "I would have exchanged those names for any other, even Sardine. Perhaps I could be called Toasty Sardine!" She loved sardines, especially on toast- very strange- but woefully so. They were her favourite snack, a very unusual choice for a child. Most children asked for crisps, but Margarine asked for sardines on cream crackers or toast.

Margarine was born into very peculiar social circumstances and without family to call her own, her situation seemed to be a rather sad one. Two weeks after her birth, Social Services became busy. She was taken into a children's home to be cared for by other people, because her mum, who had become too acquainted with intoxicating liquids, was often incapable of looking after her. She had problems remembering her own name and often forgot that she had in fact, had a baby; a baby who was a human being and needed looking after. Eventually, in the months that followed, her mum's social circumstances plummeted to such an extent that it was almost a huge relief for her that baby Margarine was to be taken away to safeguard her life. She hadn't been the best of mothers after all. On occasions, having satiated herself to an unacceptably high level of intoxication, she had forgotten to feed Margarine, not to mention the many times she had nearly drowned the unfortunate child during a bath. It was for the poor child's own safety that she had to be placed in the care of different people. It seemed as though tiny Margarine's life had been sorely affected, even before it begun, and if it ever did, it was with a jolt from a nightmare.

***

Margarine's mum was called Variella. Variella was a young woman, with no particular ambitions in life. She had dropped out of school at age 16 and run away from home. She was skinny and slightly rough on the edges, having associated with the wrong crowd for most of her young life. For years, Variella stayed with friends, shunning every positive influence from her family who reached out to her, and roaming from one place to the other, engaging in activities no human being should expose themselves to. Not surprising, Variella became pregnant.

When she was due to give birth to Margarine, Variella was so full of alcohol she couldn't find her way to the hospital. She found strength miraculously, though, to walk down her road. From there, she dragged herself to the next road, then the next. From one lamppost to the next she toddled and trudged, with disinterested and unhelpful passers-by gazing in disapproval. She was quite a sight too; tight pair of jeans trousers that gave the belly no space to breathe, cheap knee-high boots with adhesive tapes on the sides, a cigarette in one hand and a can of beer in the other. Her steps were a rhythmic clumping that betrayed great discomfort and still, no one cared to stop and help her. That was the situation though, people often didn't stop to help suspicious looking strangers no matter how troubled, for fear of being robbed or becoming victims of planned attacks. Variella must have walked for ages when she suddenly let out a loud scream. Not even an indulgence in some of her favourite food - cigarette, beer and a spoonful of frozen margarine - which she dutifully and routinely kept in her bag- could hold back the pain and throbbing she felt in her lower abdomen. A lamppost was the nearest thing to hold on for safety and stability, so she grabbed on to it with all her might. Fear gripped Variella's heart even as hope made a dash towards the road. "Will someone call an ambulance?" her mouth mumbled that which her mind wondered. Then, as if on cue, everything around her became a blur, before being finally engulfed by a tunnel of darkness. Nothing stirred, nothing spoke, neither a sneeze nor a burp provoked the silence around her. She was in total darkness, her limbs splayed at the curb where she was slumped like a sack of semi- steamed corn. When Variella awoke, she was greeted by two large, sparkling eyes; watery and innocent, but curious - looking eyes. Those shiny beautiful eyes stared into the face of what was left of her mother, not knowing whether her future laid inside herself or in the hands of the disconnected eyes looking back at her. Born, to a mother who couldn't make out that the pair of eyes staring at her were in fact her newly born baby, that future looked very dim indeed. Variella couldn't remember a thing about how she got to the hospital. It was worrying that she had in fact had a child; a human being; a helpless little bundle whose survival depended on her.

Variella had been rescued by strangers who felt humane enough to over-look her obnoxious and suspicious state and rather consider the plight of her unborn child. They had rescued her in time and managed to alert a hospital nearby. They had then carefully lifted her into their car and rushed her for emergency care. Margarine was surprisingly born without a single scar or scratch. Ironically, her tiny organs and other body parts had been safely preserved from all the toxic elements Variella had indulged her appetite in, during her pregnancy. Still, the future looked bleak for Margarine indeed. When the strangers brought Variella to the hospital, they were kind enough to leave their names and contact information, and further agreed to fill out a form as next of kin. It appeared that Variella had no one to stand in as family and the hospital had no way of getting anyone to help her. Fortunately, before leaving the hospital, these wonderful strangers who had been such great Samaritans, requested that their phone number and address were passed on to Variella, whose name they did not know at the time. Mr. and Mrs. Dickson had been very kind to stop and lend a hand. It wasn't every day you saw a drunk and collapsed pregnant woman lying supine near a curb. Variella was subsequently discharged from hospital but not before the hospital had managed to gather various contributions of nappies, baby clothes and other baby essentials for her to take along. Variella left the hospital, completely unprepared for the journey into motherhood. She named her baby Margarine, simply because she had developed an insatiable craving for the pale-yellow spread and over the course of her pregnancy, had become quite close to it; not that it added any flavour to her life. Logically, therefore, she felt a loyalty to build a most cherished memory for her much-loved fatty friend, so her daughter was to be called Margarine. For a woman who was often mixed up in her steps, not knowing whether to walk forward, backward or to hop, Variella had a certain sincerity about her, with a polished sense of loyalty. Thoughtfully, she decided to show her gratitude to the strangers by naming them Godparents to her daughter, though she hardly knew them. With this decision, she made her choice, a choice which was to be the most sensible one she had made in her

entire life thus far. She had definitely defined
Margarine's future with an authoritative stamp,
oblivious to herself; even if she was unaware that
Mr. and Mrs. Dickson often lived abroad.

When the kind-hearted couple were later contacted

8

by the hospital with the news of their conferred status, they couldn't be more pleased. You see, now in their mid-fifties, the Dicksons had long given up on their wish for a child of their own. Biologically, they were healthy human beings, however, life had handed them some very harsh realities and in their thirty-eight years of marriage, had saddled them with six birth misfortunes. As a consequence, a previous insensitive neighbour had cruelly labeled them 'the witch and wizard of Barrenfield'. The Dicksons' desire to move abroad was therefore instigated by one last straw eighteen years earlier when they lost their premature twin boys to pneumonia. Yes, they have had their fair share of nature's grits and yet they were the most lovely and pleasant people to have the great fortune of encountering. Having Margarine as a Goddaughter was more than they could have hoped for. Indeed, you could sincerely say that the one tiny sensible thing Variella did was making this decision and also ensuring she stayed in touch with the Dicksons so that when she had to go into rehabilitation - which was inevitable and quite frequently too- she let them know what could happen with Margarine. The Dicksons were fairly informed on Margarine's wellbeing and were notified whenever Margarine was moved to a different carer. Margarine was like a yo-yo, always being moved hither and thither and never stabilised for too long. This worried the Dicksons who often discussed her and made arrangements to see her as frequently as possible, when they were in England. As Margarine became of age she, however, often, refused to see them. She would agree to a visit and when the Dicksons arrived, she would change her mind. This was a regular occurrence and appeared as though margarine was playing up. But as far as she was concerned Mr. And Mrs. Dickson were strangers who could make promises and then break them. They may look all splendid and caring and even love her for a while but she was confused what it all meant. They could take her away to yet another unfamiliar home which she might grow to hate. Each time she had to stay with new people, she felt jittery in her bones. Her limbs felt drained of all energy and then her fingers and toes went into a funny tingle. This is when she would feel a kind of numbness followed by a wave of tension which flooded her spine and, froze her to a spot for some seconds. Margarine kept this all to herself. You would have imagined that such painful experiences were enough to make Margarine a little more caring of others, less unruly and slightly more willing to acquiesce to any good natures inside her. After all, isn't there some truth in the notion that painful personal experiences have a way of making people a bit kinder and more thoughtful towards others? But no, not Margarine. Her inner natures wanted nothing to do with how others felt, so she was rather willing to pretend she didn't care and instead suffer all the paralysis in the world. Inside her little body, Margarine was petrified of life. If you looked into her little pearly eyes, you would quickly realise that fear was lurking in her shadows. Yes, Margarine was too scared to report these experiences so with each minute, her mind wandered deeply into darkness; darkness created by loneliness and a sense of rejection; rejection brought on by a conglomeration of social issues and patterns of upbringing surrounding her early childhood. Hundreds of ideas and doubt flickers danced around her thoughts, deeply strangling joy from her soul. Thousands of ridiculing and mocking laughter rang in her ears, with sharp clanging sounds and disturbing shrieks, torturous enough to drive a person insane. So, having felt all alone for a very long time, Margarine convinced herself that no one cared. It seemed that the lack of a stable home had knocked Margarine's confidence really badly. Was it her fault that her mum was an alcoholic? Why is her father not around? Does she have any family? Are all her family like her mum? Where are her family? And what is family anyway? These were some of the questions that played on Margarine's delicate mind and seemed to also plague the other children she shared a home with. This mental battle with confidence, self-esteem and other psychological traumas were debilitating and terrifying. Margarine was gaining a bad labelling: She was naughty. She was thoughtless. She was mean. But Margarine was a troubled soul. Margarine was an issue that needed to be solved.

If only she had been offered some therapy or support, something could have been done earlier but as that didn't happen, each fostering experience intensified the numbness; the numbness which was gradually developing into a kind of temporary paralysis. Margarine grew worse and became even more lost in her soul. She was deeply lonely, yet young as she was, she continued to endure this suffering. Alone.

2

Who needs a family?

Margarine did not like it anywhere. She had no safe family member she could live with. Her dad was in prison for constantly taking other people's stuff without asking. There was this incident where he entered a jewellery shop and helped himself to a complete collection of gold watches. The law didn't smile at that so he ended up in prison. Having been captured by the grips of the law meant that he hadn't made acquaintance with Margarine yet. Variella, her mother, was still undecided as to whether to stay off intoxicating elements and be a responsible mother, or to lead a careless life, going through the now familiar cyclical pattern of homelessness, rehabilitation, and social sheltering. Her story so far, just like Margarine's dad, remained neither appealing nor alluring. She was receiving treatment for her constant misuse of substances and hadn't seen her daughter since she was 6 months old. Margarine was a loner from birth, not by her choice, but by the recklessness of her parents. In the mornings, she drew the tiny frame you may call her body, to the window of the bedroom she shared with two other children, greeted the chirping birds with questions and at night, hid behind the bedroom window curtain, sadly gazing at the stars for answers. She was looked after by complete strangers with whom she had neither the inclination to nor the intention of bonding. As a young child, she could not see herself bestowed with a silver spoon when she knew that she would probably wake up in the dead of the night drenched in sweat, having had yet another nightmarish dream, a more crippling one than the night before. She would dread closing her eyes again for fear she might be swallowed into a deep revolting tunnel with ghostly shadows whimpering their traumas away. Margarine was even scared she might go to sleep at night and wake up the next morning in another bed, with tormenting aliens baring their enormous, jagged teeth at her. She trembled at the thought.

At age three, Margarine could speak very clearly and eloquently. "Shush your nose," was her earliest favourite phrase and it had to be said that Margarine belaboured the phrase. Everyone - from delivery men to gas meter readers, stretching to dogs - was told to "shush your nose" by Margarine. "The one good thing about being a 'Cops', is that I can talk from morning to evening, and then start all over again," Margarine often boasted. "Listen now Margarine, I don't want you going through to the kitchen. You know it's not safe when the floor has just been mopped, and also particularly because there may be sharp things lying about in places," cautioned Mrs. Wellies, the resident social worker. Margarine, who usually paid no heed to any degree of caution at all, was, in a matter of micro-seconds of that instruction, doing exactly what she had been warned against. You would have thought that any child needed just one or two reminders or perhaps a couple of warnings to understand that a situation was dangerous. Well, no, not Margarine. She often needed six, seven or perhaps ten warnings and even that had to be followed by a scream, a yell, a pleading, some bribing, a chain of blackmailing, and finally physical removal and a deposit in some place called a naughty corner! To add insult to injury, Margarine loved day-dreaming. Poor old Mrs. Wellies didn't stand a chance when little Margarine lent herself to a bout of day-dreaming. Why? Well, you might think that day-dreaming kept people disengaged from their surroundings and from physical activities, right? Perhaps so, but not with Margarine. Her day-dreaming involved a chain of physical consequences: there were usually arguments with half the children in the home, incidents of running under a dining table and refusing to see any sense; a series of biting; hair pulling; shoulder grabbing; thick fat slaps on faces and finally neck scratching laced with a certain perfected deafening screech before a most definite show of defiance with door banging. "Put a lid on it, Margarine, please keep it down!" her carers often pleaded. However, this usually fell on deaf ears. Margarine never put a lid on it. In fact she let the lid off as much as she wanted so she was often heard instructing and screaming at the other children, rumbling on like a pot of boiling potatoes. At her worst she would bite anyone and anything that got in her way. Margarine was an expert biter. Her bite had a force similar to a crocodile's bite. Her jaws clasped on her victims with such a snap it always took three adults to pry her mouth open. This was definitely more than an issue. This was pure annihilation! Margarine was schooled in biting. She bit adults, children, and animals. Adults feared any closeness to her. Children run from her. Animals whimpered at her approach. Dogs and cats especially, stayed well away from her. Rumour had it that once, inside the local grocery shop, Margarine had grabbed a chihuahua by the neck and was about to go for the kill when the shop keeper let out a most spine-tingling scream.

Margarine was also a skilled tantrum thrower; she could whip up such terrible tantrums at the most unimaginable times that she absolutely frightened the adults who looked after her. Margarine was a very loud child. "I don't think it's fair on us and the other children. One can hardly think," Mrs. Wellies, spoke to no one in particular. "We had three missed calls on the phone the other day, all because Margarine was on the loose," she continued as she walked into the tea room. Mrs. Wellies went to make a cup of tea and in her soliloquizing, didn't pay attention to what she was doing. "Shifty Shenanigans, mother of a mussel!" she spat out. "Salt!" she squawked. "Margarine!" she yelled. She angrily looked around and sighed. "No Margarine?" she gritted. Of course, there was no 'Margarine' in the tea room. She had put salt in her tea, and she had done it because Margarine was invading her thoughts! Again! Mrs. Wellies walked to a chair and sat stiffly with rampant murmuring oozing out of her mouth: "I don't know why we can't ship her off to Neptune or some other planet! Certainly, there must be something someone could do! Or perhaps I ought to pay a visit to my nurse, my nerves may be cracking." Poor Mrs. Wellies was losing her flavour. Her patience had long hit the hard road!

Margarine was giving everyone a headache. Her behaviours were simply unsuitable for a child. Gradually, this little girl had built a terrible reputation that followed her almost everywhere she went. "There's a Margarine issue again," Mrs. Wellies often reported over the phone.

One day Margarine had jumped through an open bedroom window into a garden with the aim of landing on a trampoline. She had missed, and was heading for a free-fall when luckily, the gardener – who was well aware of the Margarine situation- heard a sound, looked up just in time to see Margarine flying down. "Ginormous gabbling giraffe!" he screamed, catching her in mid-air before any damage could be done. Margarine was always on the move. She was a lively little girl with a very curious nature. In many ways, she was an extremely insightful and astute child, but this was very often betrayed by her lack of sensitivity towards others. Her thoughts converted into actions, at the speed of lightning, so often in the middle of breakfast, lunch, dinner or something in-between, Margarine rose and set herself up to some mischief. She wandered into wardrobes, got lost in duvets or figured out how a locked washing machine door opened and then got her tiny frame inside the washer. One day, she caused a great scare in the children's home when she sneaked into the medical room after the key was mistakenly left in the keyhole. Locating a medicine cabinet, little Miss Cops helped herself to nearly a full bottle of paracetamol syrup. Once again, she was found just in time, taken for medical attention and tragedy was averted. Having lived in different homes made Margarine's social and emotional life very unstable. She didn't enjoy living with so many different people every few months as this made it difficult for her to form meaningful roots. Her mind was overtaken with images of human beings in various forms, shapes, sizes and colours. A child couldn't be more confused than Margarine was. Sadly, this confusion was like a big shadow constantly hovering over her, sometimes scarily reaching out to suffocate her. It took away her sense of belonging and safety, leaving her feeling like an imposter each time. If Margarine's behaviours and attitudes towards everything weren't so bad, she may have managed to endear herself to at least one foster carer, who might have been willing to foster her for longer periods. That way, she would not have been in and out of the children's home with every fresh blowing of wind. Margarine was only a child but she often portrayed herself as a selfish, thoughtless, cruel, devious and careless child. Most of the time, she was impervious to the feelings of others, more than one would expect from most children her age. Even though she was still a child, everyone was terrified of her. Her behaviours could have led to dangerous consequences and that caused great worry for the people who looked after her. How could you possibly feel safe around a child who spat into other people's food, flushed keys down toilets and tried to turn toys into a Sunday roast by putting them in the oven and setting the oven on? Yes, Margarine had numerous undisputed accolades, none of which was positive. Getting angry and pretending to poke a child's eye out or threatening to wrench their tongue seemed like the norm for her. And though they were dangerous threats from a child, she hadn't carried them out so at least they were much preferred to putting spiders in people's sandwiches, or bath gel on toothbrushes. Margarine was the epitome of a blend of recalcitrance and insanity so as a result, every few weeks, she had a different place to stay; none of these was somewhere she could call 'home'. Thirteen foster carers later as her fourth birthday approached, Margarine had to be relocated into a different children's home, a permanent one for children in care.

Mr. and Mrs. Dickson were in and out of foster and children's homes at every opportunity, visiting Margarine as though they were her parents. They loved her and were determined to look out for her for as long as they could. The Dicksons passionately committed to this venture. It was a dream come true for them to have been made Godparents and they were not about to take that for granted.

As always, little Margarine didn't care at all. She was clearly not interested in anything the Dicksons had to offer. Life was not stopping for her, and neither was she going to give a thought to what anybody else wanted. "If life was so good, where were her parents then?" Margarine often asked herself. She didn't realise that she was the topic of discussion among the other children in the home where it was common assertion that "Margarine was the luckiest of all the children." After all, "she had the good fortune of Godparents who cared enough to visit her." Margarine was not moved by the devotion and care towards her, and she didn't fail to let everyone, including the Dicksons, know her thoughts. She didn't trust them and that was settled in her mind.

***

The Dicksons never gave up on Margarine. They sent her gifts on every birthday, at Christmas, Easter and any other excuse they could come up with. It seemed as if they were buying Margarine's affection. However, when their gestures continued regardless of her refusal to acknowledge them, she started thinking that perhaps she ought to give them a chance. As fortune would have it, one Tuesday a few weeks after her 6th birthday, Margarine received a letter from her Godparents. They had returned to England to settle permanently and were interested in seeing her more frequently. This time, Margarine was accommodating and so Mr. and Mrs. Dickson were allowed to visit her more frequently at the foster home where she had most recently been placed. It was a welcomed change for Margarine, who had experienced one too many self-inflicting traumas to keep count. Yes, Margarine Cops had gone through the 'poke your finger in a plug hole and receive an electric shock for real' experience; she had overcome the 'attempt climbing an eight feet high obstacle, and in the process fall and bang your head' episode; not to mention her 'intentionally sprain an ankle, bruise your chin and get some attention' catastrophic ordeal. She was now ready to play 'four-in-a-row', 'guess who' 'ludo', 'snakes and ladders' or 'scrabble', simple games for children. The Dicksons regularised their visits and soon expressed an interest in fostering Margarine. That presented another hurdle. One would have thought that Maya would have jumped at such an appealing prospect, after all as the saying goes, "beggars can't be choosers". Well, Margarine was no beggar, and she did have a choice. She didn't want to stay with the Dicksons and did not even remotely look like she was missing anything at all. She wasn't even interested in going to live with the couple even if for a short period. It looked as though her anxiety and confused state had more effect on her than was noticeable at first glance. The many movements in her young life had somewhat crippled her senses and erected alarm bells where jingles should be sounding. Sensing Margarine's tension, Miss. Chintwit, her 'case manager', assured her that her stay with the Dicksons was only temporary, a trial period for her to make up her mind. "The Dicksons have a pony," she had whispered into Margarine's ears. Poor Mrs. Chintwit would jump through hoops just to be rid of the notorious Margarine. With eyeballs nearly bulging out of their sockets, Margarine ran as fast as her miniature feet could lift her and within a twinkle, returned with a packed suitcase; a smile spread across her face as though she had eaten a clownfish.

Margarine went to live with the Dicksons, unaware that her life was just about to take a sharp turn; for the better. Her Godparents took a liking to her instantly, regardless of some of her unconventional behaviours. Margarine was always everywhere and yet neither here nor there. Her mind was as higgledy-piggledy as her clothes that lay scattered on her bedroom floor. She was into everything and seemed to have a long list of mischievous assignments to see to. Ironically, this introduced a funny twist to her personality which made her rather likeable to the Dicksons. Mrs. Dickson nicknamed her 'Little Flappity Maya' and soon her name Margarine changed to Flappity Maya in the Dickson household. The Dicksons loved every fiber of hair on their Flappity Maya and offered to extend their fostering period, exploring the possibilities of helping Maya refine her ways. They felt that she needed lots of love and care and could only fully appreciate that if she stayed in one home for longer durations. Maya desperately wanted to be treated as a child, brought up in a normal way and not allowed to 'take over or terrify people' all the time. She was just an ordinary child with extraordinary problems. "Children need nurturance, lots of nurturance and that's what Maya will get," Mrs. Dickson told Maya's 'case manager' during one of her visits. It took a long time for Maya to realise that Mr. and Mrs. Dickson were different; that they were genuinely interested in her welfare and were ready to make adjustments in their lives in order to get her assimilated into her new life. Reluctantly, Maya came to accept this new pattern that her life took. Within a year of fostering her, Mr. and Mrs. Dickson decided to adopt Maya. Variella had, a few years gone, signed documents to make this an interest worth considering. Now, it was a possibility the Dicksons were eager to explore. They spoke to the fostering and adoption agency, sought legal advice, made all the necessary preparations and when all documentations were completed, arrangements were made for the Dickson to have Maya as their daughter. Following that, they sought further guidance on changing Maya's name and so with Maya's approval, they changed her name from Margarine Cops to Maya Dickson. Maya understood that biologically, she was still a Cops, but socially and legally, she was now a Dickson. Maya also quickly understood that she was now going to live permanently with Mr. and Mrs. Dickson. She was secretly delighted, overjoyed, ecstatic and over the moon. Amazingly, Flappity Maya had also taken a great liking to the Dicksons, though she did not express it openly. However, being Maya, she made a fuss. In fact she made such a big fuss it appeared as though she was being kidnapped. After nearly exhausting everyone, she eventually calmed down. Miss Margarine Cops became Miss Flappity Maya Dickson. By this time Maya, little as she was, had gained quite a reputation for her screaming and biting, something the Dicksons were determined to work on.

The Dicksons became Maya's legal guardians and were very pleased to have her as a permanent addition to their family and to their home.

Maya had attended Pebbleyard Nursery for a term and in September of that year, had progressed into Green Arch Primary School.

Having moved in permanently with the Dicksons, Maya started a new school: Mayston Way Infant School. The school was near to where she now lived, but the change of environment didn't seem to make much difference for this tempestuous and volatile child.

Within weeks of joining the school, she had scratched two children on their faces and nearly bitten a teacher's thumb off. Maya was taken through various assessments by the school family worker and special needs officer to ascertain her learning and behaviour needs. Still, she remained adamantly unchanged in her ways.

Finally, a decision was made to grant her short counselling sessions to help her understand and cope with the many traumatic changes that had and were still occurring in her young life. The sessions were also designed to formally introduce Maya to certain boundaries necessary for her social integration and cohesion within the school environment and in her new home. This was meant to give Maya a smooth transition towards an easier life.

Maya was not happy with that decision. "Why didn't grown-ups listen?" she wondered. "How could I be offered counselling when all the other children are walking about?" she questioned. "After all, I am not the problem, they are!" she grunted. One dared not look at the unhappy face of this little girl. In such moods, she gritted and grunted like a piglet and wore a very long face. Settling in with Mr. and Mrs. Dickson was a herculean task for Maya and the struggle that ensued in the first few months was tiring for the Dicksons. It was difficult understanding and meeting Maya's emotional needs so they had to deploy various strategies to reach out to her, including hugging her and taking lots of photos together as a family. Knowing that Maya lacked emotional bonding with her parents, the Dicksons were very patient with her and made numerous attempts at getting Variella to visit her but to no avail. Variella's name was beginning to sound, smell and taste like unpalatable food in Maya's mouth. It appeared that the mere mention of her name stirred up nausea in the little girl's throat.

Poor Maya didn't like people physically getting too close. She detested the word ' hugs'. She didn't give hugs! And she most definitely didn't like being hugged! Maya didn't even like seeing people hug and would often get into tantrums and fits if she witnessed any. Mrs. Dickson often hugged her nonetheless and wasn't frazzled by Maya's frenzies.

A child like Maya often waved the flag of alarm wherever she went. Again and again, she was caught in dangerous situations, so people often stayed on the alert in her presence. Wherever Maya went, a Margarine issue presented itself. With her notoriety, it came as no surprise that as the school term rolled by, Maya brought little gifts home. First, she said they were from the teachers for her good behaviours, then they came from the other children because she had been kind to them. Mrs. Dickson, aware of the myriad of mischievous deeds lodged in Maya's head, suspected that she wasn't telling the truth and a visit to the school confirmed her suspicion. Maya had started taking other people's properties. If she was challenged, she fought and bit the person. Mrs. Dickson's neighbours also noticed that when Maya went over for a visit, things suddenly went missing; little things and big things. It was even said that one day a guitar went missing when Maya left a neighbour's house.

"If Maya had been a teenager, I'm sure she would have been spending her evenings in police cells," a very worried Mrs. Dickson shared with her husband. Mr. Dickson looked at his wife thoughtfully. Peering down his spectacles, he cast a sideways glance at Maya, who was sat with books, reluctantly completing her homework.

There had been a lot of rustling in the Dickson household since Maya joined the family, and sadly it appeared as though all of that was rooted in Maya. Neighbours observed that the very cheerful Dicksons seem to now survive on wind and prayer. Nonetheless, the Dicksons persevered with their Flappity Maya.

After what seemed like a lot of thunder and lightning, Maya finally showed signs of settling into school. She toned down from her frenetic ways and behaved slightly more 'acceptably'. This was difficult but she soon got the hang of it.

Even though there were lots of toys to play with and lots more to steal for home, it still wasn't the same as playing with the other children. Maya wanted to play with them more regularly but that didn't often happen so instead, she stayed in the 'home corner' of the classroom or playground, in her own little world, and played all by herself. Sometimes she went on the slides and played with a few of the boys who didn't mind. At other times she sat on the bouncy hoppers and watched the other children play happily, secretly yearning to scratch their faces and bite their arrogant noses off. Her favourite activity was skating. She fell off her skater a few times but enjoyed skating so much that she didn't mind the knee scrapes.

Mayston Way Infant School wasn't great fun for
Maya, because she couldn't always have her way,
but it was a good change from the foster homes and
the children's homes. It had been a lot of months
now since she started the school and looking back,
Maya knew even if she didn't admit it, that she
liked having a permanent residence with people she
could almost see as parents.

***

By the summer of Year Two, Maya's behaviours had begun showing signs of domestication. "Hello, my name is Maya, what's yours?" Mrs. Dickson often heard her whispering to herself. On weekends, she routinely asked Mrs. Dickson, "Can Tinsel come for a play date tomorrow? She would be so disappointed if you said no." "Yes," Mrs. Dickson usually said, indulging Maya's sense of play, "Tinsel can come for a play date and so can Cinderella, Tiana, Bella and all your other dolls."

Gradually, Maya progressed to Mayston Way Junior School. Junior School wasn't that different, just a bit more grown up. Most of the pupils had progressed with her from the Infant School and that meant that in her view most of the children who were supposedly mean, and bossy were still around. The few friendly ones who played with her a few times had stopped, scared of being seen regularly playing with her and for fear of being picked on. They were also afraid of having their hair pulled by Maya, or worse still, getting bitten too.

Maya was nearly eight years and knew that any wrong behaviours could have more serious consequences for her at that point, than they did in Infant School. Desperate to fit in, she began identifying with her good senses. She still entangled herself in the occasional fights but these were now becoming rare and a luxury so she chose her moments carefully. Deciding which people to fight and which fights were not worth taking up was hard work, but Maya persevered.

Whenever she gave in to the temptations, she often tried to explain away the unacceptable behaviours but the teachers who seemed to have had enough, paid no heed to her words. It was an established fact that Maya didn't have any learning difficulties, just a tendency towards making wrong choices. Her behaviours therefore needed improvement so the school decided to inculcate in her a continuous awareness of the consequences of not making reflective decisions. In view of this, she was signed into a 'social skills' group organised by the school pastoral care team. She was also assigned a learning mentor to help her engage with her school learning in a less disruptive way. She attended the skills group every school day for half an hour and had the learning mentor to support her regularly in and out of class. She hated it all. Week after week, Maya attended the group session and each time she hated it more. Mrs. Dickson encouraged her to remain positive about it. She even offered to attend some of the sessions if that was going to help. Maya didn't welcome that idea. It was bad enough as things stood. She didn't want any name- calling and cooing at play time. Maya thought that some of the children enjoyed seeing others suffer - not that she counted herself as one - and they would definitely pounce on this opportunity to make her life more miserable. "No!" she said emphatically to Mrs. Dickson, "I would rather go alone." So, Maya attended every week and every week the experience was more torturous, nothing positive, in Maya's opinion. "The boys in the group are bullies and the other girls are very selfish," she reported to Mrs. Dickson. She explained how in one session, all the children were paired up and asked to share ideas and talk about their feelings. Then they were given sheets of paper to show these feelings in drawings. Maya was paired with a boy who, instead of working, kept making mean faces at her. When she tried to tell the teacher, she received a telling off for not being friendly. That afternoon, with great sadness, she told her Godmother what had happened: "Miss McTufy was not interested in what I had to say. She didn't care about what happened to me at all, not even when Dany intentionally knocked a pot of paint onto my drawings, messing them up completely!"

Maya went quiet. Then she resumed her narrative, "I refused to cry and told myself that if I didn't get out of the group before the next half-term things were going to get worse. What do you think?" she asked Mrs. Dickson who was trying hard to conceal her joy on hearing Maya's frustrations. Mr. Dickson, who was watching the news, stopped to join in the conversation. He could also instantly tell that Maya was getting tired of the bad reputation. She wanted out! And he was happy to contribute some suggestions. "Are you scared of ending up without any friends?" he asked Maya. Maya knew the answer to that question, and it disturbed her. For the first time, the implication of that truth hit home like a dart on a bullseye! She was awakened to how her life could roll downwards if she didn't make an effort. Instantly, it dawned on her that even though the social skills group was meant to help her, if she stayed in the group, she could be a lot closer to the bullying and other mean behaviours and that wasn't going to help her. She listened to Mr. Dickson's suggestions and in the days that followed, made more efforts at being even more pleasant towards the other children. She even went an extra mile and smiled rather than get back at them. This was hard work. But this was her exit ticket. Maya's learning mentor was a tremendous help too and encouraged her regularly. Maya listened and followed each encouragement and guidance as though her life depended on them. And in a way, her life did depend on these! Besides she didn't want to face constantly going to the head teacher's office or the school meeting room for that matter. She wanted everyone to just leave her alone. Yes, desperation had crept in, and Maya was ready to change her ways. The Dicksons cracked a smile at each other during dinner one evening, after another conversation with Maya revealed that finally, a glimmer of hope may be trotting their way.

3

You may call it a hobby

Maya started Year Five feeling more hopeful. Her list of problems was just about manageable. She was performing well in school and being friendlier to most people. After school, she couldn't wait to dash off with Mrs. Dickson. Going home had become something she looked forward to, more often, mostly because Mr. Dickson always had a plate of sardines on cream crackers judiciously set on the dining table, waiting for her. On Friday nights she cherished the movie treats she received with a large cinema-size bucket of popcorn and a 1500ml bottle of cream soda which made her burp disgracefully like an impoverished prawn. She loved it!

Maya was enjoying her home life and as a result, she was having an equally enjoyable school life. She could do her nine times table, read books two years above her age, and had enough interest in the other subjects to keep her going steadily through school. Being Flappity Maya, she still believed that any trouble she faced in school was because of someone's negligence. Other people had to take the blame for her troubles! There was however one significant development in Maya's life. During the last four years she had been in school, she had taken to skating to keep her from feeling lonely. You may call this a hobby. She often skated all by herself in their garden and in Infant School she had often skated at lunch and morning breaks to keep herself occupied.

At the start of Junior School she refrained from skating in school for fear of being picked on but often returned to it as soon as she reached home. She attended skating classes and was a competent and skilled skater for her level and age. Four years on, she had developed a flair for the sports and was particularly interested in dance skating. This brought a great boost to her confidence, an activity that took away idleness and served as an excellent companion. She talked to herself during skating, reprimanded herself and regularly reminded herself of how she could avoid getting into trouble.

As if by design, one day all the children at school were told to bring their bicycles, skateboards and scooters for a play time competition. This was like the opportunity Maya had been waiting for; to show that there was another side to her, an admirable side. She wanted everyone to see a different Maya. After all, she wasn't called Flappity Maya for nothing. She decided to take the skating shoes she had received from her Godparents for her ninth birthday. Those shoes could merge with her feet in a way that beat all explanations and she loved it and was very grateful indeed. Perhaps this was the opportunity for a new chapter for her. Yesterday, they had gone dinning out- a wonderful treat from Mr. Dickson- but whilst there, Mrs. Dickson had gritted her teeth at her for not being grateful. She had wanted apple pie for dessert, but the waitress had mistakenly brought strawberry cheesecake. Maya loved cheesecake so it came as a complete surprise when she wore a grumpy robe and complained to the death. At that point, Mrs. Dickson had had enough and chided her severely. "Now, Maya," Mrs. Dickson had pointed at her, "even you know that this behaviour is disgraceful, and you must be ashamed. Sometimes, in life you get handed lemons instead of cherries. What you do is not to squirt the lemon juice in people's eyes!" "I don't have a lemon, and I won't squirt lemon juice in people's eyes," Maya was about to say. But the look on Mrs. Dickson's face, and the tightness on her jawline, squelched every sentence Maya had formulated. She consequently shut her mouth! Mrs. Dickson had paused and engaged Maya's attention; "no! you say 'thank you' to life, and then you make lemonade and sell it to make money or share with other people!" Mrs. Dickson sternly made her point and Maya, even though confused about the need to sell lemonade or even share it with others, knew straight away that she was going to carry that message in her head forever. "Squirting lemon juice and selling lemonade!" she still looked baffled. "The waitress had bought strawberry cheesecake. How did Mrs. Dickson get apple pie mixed up with lemon? One never knows with these adults," she concluded.

 Bringing her mind back to the present, that being her immaculate bedroom, she knelt to examine her beautiful skating shoes on the shoe rack next to her chest of drawers; they were adorable, and she was going to skate for everyone to see. She was going to enter her little world and shine. Skating was her refuge and now skating will be the gateway to establish a new identity for her; a lighthouse to lead her on a more positive path. That day was about the happiest day in Maya's life. Well, apart from the day she stepped into her Godparent's house; that had been pure joy. She had never been in a massive house like that before in all her life.

Imagine a huge, detached house with five large bedrooms and she had one all to herself. Her room was beautifully decorated, and her bed was so large she could have hosted five other children to sleep in it. She adored the garden and the swimming pool and felt very fortunate indeed to have such well-placed people looking after and bringing her up. It had been a few years now but looking back, Maya felt a little ungrateful for all the fuss she made the day she heard the fostering news. Not surprising, she remembered that Mrs. Chintwit had to concoct all sorts of tails to convince her. She had been insistent on fussing non-stop, and it appeared that a little devil had set itself loose in her. Whoever heard of anyone making a fuss at being given an opportunity in life? Still, she had been younger and didn't realize the deep implications of her actions even if at the time she understood that what she was doing was wrong.

Maya arrived at school the next morning, glowing like a firefly and chirping like a parrot. All through the morning's lessons, she struggled to focus, excited in anticipation of getting into her skating shoes. All she wanted to do was to prance and twirl and skate. When the time approached, Maya did not let herself down. She performed her skating so beautifully she won everyone's heart with her many self-developed skating styles, something her flappity nature creatively encouraged. The teachers saw her in a different light and the supposed bullies even wanted to be friends with her. The classified selfish girls were too proud to acknowledge defeat, but Maya knew they too admired her. Maya's performance completely enthralled the whole school. The next thing she knew was she had been selected to represent her school at the termly zones skating competitions. This was to be the first of three competitions she took part in before reaching Year 6. "Wow," she thought, feeling very fulfilled. A new chapter of her life was unfolding right before her eyes. It was unbelievable.

Maya had never been chosen for anything before in her whole life. She was fascinated and jittery but was not one to bow out of a challenge. With her heart thumping and bouncing in her chest, she went into her skating competitions in full plunge and she loved them. All the contests were held in the sports halls across various regions and were a great source of fun for Maya. The contestants were judged on skating abilities and creativity, and as this was Maya's niche, it was very easy for her. She had been skating for a significant number of years. She knew how to always produce her best and enchant the crowd, so she always placed high. Not surprising, she also made new friends.

The most fascinating of this new friendship development was a boy named Carwyn. "Hi, I think your skating rocks," said a soft voice as Maya sat under a shady tree during one lunch break, reading a thick red book about Pippi Longstocking, one of her favourite stories, and minding her own business. When Maya didn't respond the voice continued, "I noticed that you don't cycle so well, so let's make a deal. You teach me skating and I'll teach you cycling." Maya turned around slowly to where the intruding voice came from. She found herself sternly looking into a face full of freckles just like Mr. Dickson's. Her first instinct was to laugh. She stopped herself quick enough and instead softened her face and smiled awkwardly. She said nothing instead she stared sheepishly. "Hi," continued the freckle-faced boy, "my name is Carwyn Driscoll and I'm in your class." "Oh wonderful news!" Maya exclaimed sarcastically. "And where do you perch? I mean where do you sit?" she blurted out before she could stop herself. Then she apologised and offered another smiled. "Hi, my name is Maya, Maya Dickson. How do you know I don't cycle well? I've never cycled at school." Carwyn wore a

44

cheeky look and responded, "of course, I've never seen you ride, I'm only making conversation." Maya relaxed. Of course, she knew who Carwyn Driscoll was. With the platter of freckles on his face screaming for attention, he was certainly hard to miss, but Maya hadn't cared. She had seen him in all her school year group photos at home but had been too engrossed in her social problems to worry about a freckle-faced boy who never answered questions in class because he was too busy being shy. Maya remembered all too well that, each time Carwyn had mastered the courage to put his hand up, she had calculatedly sprung her hand up at that same moment, and always ended up beating him to it. To her it was a game and she needed to win. Shamefully, but courageously she drew Carwyn's attention to these previous intentional pranks and apologised for all her past unfriendly behaviours towards Carwyn. As it turned out, Carwyn had not been aware of the malice. He had been too shy to realise it.

Then Maya succumbed to the nagging question on her mind. "Why do you have so many freckles on your face? I suppose you eat lots of pancakes with strawberry syrup. That's what Mr. Dickson said." Both children split into laughter. "How strange! We laughed simultaneously." Maya thought. She knew straight away that she finally had a genuine

friend. Maya and Carwyn got into a conversation
and talked endlessly. As the weeks rolled on, each
child found play times more appealing and looked
forward to it. Carwyn seemed to have broken out of
his shyness shell whilst Maya looked to have
become more enthusiastic about school, well
behaved and friendlier. During morning play, the
two friends met under the shady tree which they had
since adopted and named Freckles, and played
'rock, paper, scissors' and as Carwyn often won,
Maya had to carry his water bottle after lunch
almost every lunch time. She also had to balance his
lunch box on her head for ten steps without
dropping it. Of course, Maya always dropped the
lunch box before she took her first step and the two
friends would then laugh hysterically. The duo
became the best of friends to the point that the first
of the two who was faster to the playground sat
under their friendship tree and waited till the other
joined. Both children were truly transformed, but
Maya, more. At last, they both had someone to look
on as friends, but more so for Maya. Her world was
completely transformed at the realization that she
had a friend who seemed playful, kind, and sincere.
A friend who was going to play regularly with her
and teach her about not biting, attacking, fighting,
or scratching people. She would have liked a girl for
a friend so they could talk about polka dot dresses,

skating shoes, pink wallpaper, make-up, nail polish and hopscotch, and perhaps just a little bit about creepy crawlies, tractors, and the mechanics of shoe lacing. But none of the girls wanted to stay around her for more than five minutes. Apparently, they hadn't recovered from the shock of the hair- pulling and nose-biting incidents from Year two! Still, she was glad she had a friend at all.

Carwyn Driscoll was a very polite boy; a truly kind and caring child, a perfect match to help Maya take a more critical look at life. Perhaps, knowing that all children were not the same and that some acted sensibly and sensitively was the final antidote to curing the sting in Maya; Carwyn had been there all the time, all the way from Infant School. It was amazing that they should suddenly become conscious of each other at a time when she desperately needed a friend. "Wasn't it strange how in life you only saw more of something soon as you consciously noticed its existence? Is that not what grey-bearded teachers referred to as 'The Frequency Illusion'?" Maya went into closed thoughts. "What did her Godfather call the long-bearded man on T.V who was talking about this concept?" Maya couldn't remember, still she knew that it was significant to cherish her new friendship. Being an extremely shy boy had meant that Carwyn often stayed by himself. Plus, Maya had too many problems of her own to have even noticed anyone else.

Over time, Mr. and Mrs. Dickson met Mr. and Mrs. Driscoll and the two families became acquainted. The Driscolls were pleasant and polite people and occasionally asked Maya over to play with their son. Carwyn's mum often asked her along to the cinema too, which was great fun. Gradually, Maya identified a lot more goodness in herself and expanded her positive natures.

The delightful summer term had barely four weeks left before school broke off and for once Maya did not look forward to the long break. Full of cheer and bubbling over, she decided to design a holiday journal for Carwyn. "You must remember to take lots of photos during your holidays and stick them in," she instructed him when she gave him the meticulously designed journal. "And Carwyn, you must write about all the fun things you do, and you must use a gel pen." She added emphatically.

***

The holidays were long and full of fun, more fun than Maya had expected. She went away on a trip to Sweden with Mr. and Mrs. Dickson. She hadn't been to Sweden before and everything seemed so different from 'The Land of the Angles'. Even though people spoke English, Maya amused herself with a few Swedish words and phrases for polite greetings and conversations; the rest were a total mystery to her. She couldn't understand what people spoke, but she felt safe and allowed herself to be happy. The cream of her Swedish experience was swimming in the ocean at Tofta beach. Tofta beach was a majestic seafront in an outskirt of Sweden called Gotland, an eccentric and clean beach with a flamboyant attitude. Regardless of the Tofta fun, the cherry on Maya's cake was when she visited Pippiland, in Kneippbyn, a suburb of Sweden and finally stepped into Villa Villekulla, the amazing abode of Pippi Longstocking, her third favourite fictional book character who lived with her horse and monkey. Her eyes were ready to pop out of their sockets as she jumped about flappily, unable to conceal her joy. She even took a photo with Pippi, to boast around school with. She was sure Carwyn's eyes would roll in their sockets if he heard all the fun she had. Soon, it was time to return to England.

Unfortunately for Maya, when they returned to England, she couldn't invite Carwyn over to play at her house because he and his family had already left for their holiday.

Carwyn sent a postcard and some pictures from Wales and Mrs. Dickson put them in an album for

Maya. Mr. and Mrs. Dickson took Maya on a trip to Devon where they visited the beautiful Dawlish Warren beach. The seafront, greeted by the silvery bluish water and the immaculate white frothy waves was a delight and Maya got tickled each time she stepped on a seashell. She had come to develop a soft spot for beaches and was fascinated by the miles of sandy walks and splendid nature reserves with trees lusciously displayed in nature's honour.

Altogether, the summer was going well, and keeping her fingers crossed, she hoped that the fun continued. Nothing was going to spoil her joy.

Next, they made an adventurous visit to Gloucester where she toured the Cathedral tower and audaciously climbed the two hundred and sixty-nine steps up the tower and back down again, learning some very intriguing and fascinating facts. Who would have thought that notoriously unruly little Maya would oblige with pleasure, the onerous task of lifting her delicate pedals called feet onto concrete slaps and rolls called steps, whilst following an articulate and strangely dressed old man, whose over-grown white beard was lengthy enough to cascade down to the very base of the steps and whose only interest was in Monks, Chapels, Gothic architecture and Church Bells? Yes, who would have thought? But yes, Maya was a reformed soul and so ninety minutes later and two wobbly legs and a bumpy tummy after, she gave herself a pat on the feet and vowed to appreciate her legs a bit more.

The summer fun continued and after two days of bed rest and couch slouching, Maya and the Dicksons were off again, this time to a Zoo. Well, that would have been a normal trip, but for the fact that Maya returned home with a monkey in her backpack; how the monkey got in there was a mystery to them, so they called the zoo out-of-office help line who were equally puzzled until a look at CCTV footage showed what had happened. One of the videos revealed two monkeys pranking a third monkey. It turned out that as Maya put her bag down to lace her trainers, the two cheeky monkeys had slid their third mate into the bag and pulled the zip up with their long fingernails. The story was hilarious but thankfully the Royal Society for the Prevention of Cruelty to Animals -RSPCA- sent two men and a van to collect the poor dolly back to the zoo, but not before Maya had attempted giving it a manicure much to the protest and dismay of Mr. and Mrs. Dickson.

Maya's fun was not truncated at all. Definitely not Maya, who carried on her summer thrills with exuberance and even got the opportunity to ride in a capsule at the London Eye. The Dicksons were exhausted to the brim; Maya on the other hand was absolutely exhilarated, fascinated at all the fun one could have in such a short space of time.

School was starting in a week when it dawned on her that they hadn't heard from Carwyn and his parents; in all her enjoyment, she had forgotten about her best friend. Mrs. Dickson took Maya over to Carwyn's house, however there was no one around. A neighbour confirmed that the house had been quiet for some weeks now. Carwyn had still not returned. He had said they were going for just a few weeks but four weeks with only one contact was worrying. Mrs. Dickson even rang Mr. Driscoll but his mobile phone was switched off.

Soon the days drew closer and it was time to resume school. At school, Maya looked in all three of the Year Six classrooms but there was no sign of Carwyn.

Settling into school in the absence of her best friend made school life slightly socially unbalanced for her. Having gone through several school years without a best friend had taught Maya an invaluable life lesson about true friendship. Even as a child, she understood that human beings needed good friends in their lives to help them develop and grow into balanced social beings. Carwyn's absence from school was therefore a source of instability and worry for Maya. Unfortunately, as the Dicksons didn't know the whereabouts of the Driscolls, they could only do very little to help. Every day after school, Mrs. Dickson took Maya on a walk to Carwyn's house, pressed their doorbell and waited patiently for some sign of life. For two weeks, they religiously pressed the Driscolls' doorbell without any response.

The weeks following were torturous for Maya. After over two long weeks of the autumn term had passed, the Headteacher, Mr. Spouts, announced at assembly that he had some bad news. "The Driscolls had been involved in a car accident on their return journey from Wales and were in a hospital," he spoke calmly; "as a result, the school was not certain whether Carwyn Driscoll could rejoin them." Mr. Spout requested a minute of silent prayer for the Driscolls but Maya had heard enough. She couldn't believe her ears and she didn't have the strength to withhold the flood of emotions that took over her. She felt paralysed to the spot for a couple of seconds, then broke into a scream. She wailed and cried uncontrollably, running out of the assembly hall before any of the adults could reach her. She didn't remember what happened next but for three days Maya was off sick from school, totally traumatised. The school counsellor and the learning mentor worked closely with Mrs. Dickson to help Maya deal with the shock and assured her that they would stay in contact with the hospital where Carwyn and his family were being cared for. Maya felt it was unfair to lose the very first true friend she had made so far in her entire life. However, the school assured her that it was not all bad news seeing as the Driscolls were still alive and could always reconnect even if Carwyn didn't come back to the school.

Year Six didn't start well and Maya could only endure the school life she had newly come to truly enjoy. Halfway through the school year Maya's desire for learning and for school waned. Not surprising, she lost her concentration for skating.

She missed her best friend and felt disconnected from the rest of her class. Mr. and Mrs. Dickson knew that the sanity of the family was under threat and Maya needed regular monitoring. Her disengagement meant that preparing for her Year Six S.A.T.s exams became a drill and a constant battle.

With the help of her Godparents and the school pastoral team, Maya received enough support to enable her re-engage with her studies and rediscover her creativity. She was able to stay socially connected with different people and interact with them appreciably but finding a new best friend was too far-fetched. The school lost communication with the Driscolls and the regular update for Maya ceased. This was disturbing and it meant that Maya didn't have much to hold on to, for assurance. She had to move on, she had no choice. So she forged on, like a flaking shadow.

While for most of Year Six going on a residential trip was the thing to die for, Maya didn't particularly share the same sentiments. Still distraught, she opted out.

Poor Maya! You would have thought that the huddle of losing her best friend was enough. After all, how much grit can life feed an eleven-year-old child? But no! Maya hadn't had the last of her troubles yet.

Late one afternoon, she returned from school to find their house surrounded by a string of police cars, the fire brigade and an ambulance; sirens blaring at their loudest and their normally quiet neighbourhood transformed into a cinema square; except that there was no big screen and no film to watch. No, it was not that jolly. It was a truly dreadful situation. It turned out that Mr. Dickson had been mowing the back garden when suddenly the electric plugs started emitting sparks. As he reached to turn off the power on the wall, he had been electrocuted and the sparks had set off a fire. Mrs. Dickson had been taking a nap in an upstairs room and was woken by her husband's scream. Some of the neighbours must have heard the scream too, and possibly seen smoke from the fire, because somebody had called the ambulance and the fire brigade.

This was the last straw that broke the camel's back. Mrs. Dicksons at this point decided that everyone needed a change. No, they didn't need a holiday. What they needed was something more: a fresh start.

The end of the school year came as a relief rather

than a celebration. Maya attended the end-of-school assembly only because she needed to. After lots of convincing from Mr. and Mrs. Dickson she also agreed to attend the 'Year Six Leavers' party. She explained that the only reason she made that decision was to please her Godparents. Still, she refused to hug anyone whatsoever, not even when she said her goodbyes on the last day of school.

4

New life or is it?

After repairing the damage to their house, the Dicksons established their decision to move away so just before the summer school break, they put their house up for sale. They were relocating to another part of the country to give Maya an opportunity to revive her interests and start over. With the situation of the house fire, Carwyn and all the events she had experienced in her young life so far, Mr. and Mrs. Dickson felt that only a totally fresh environment could give Maya a clean start;

and they needed one too. They needed to move to a completely new county and region.

Maya wanted to attend the local Grammar School where they were relocating to, so the Dicksons submitted a new secondary school application rather hurriedly and Maya, due to her mitigating circumstances was allowed to sit a late Selective Secondary School Entrance Test so that she could be considered for a school placement. Having turned over a new leaf, she decided to put her mind to it and do the best she could, and she did. She passed the test and gained admission to South Wilts Grammar School for Girls.

Meanwhile, the Dicksons were able to purchase a

large house in a quaint village in Wiltshire, in a peaceful and friendly-looking neighbourhood. The house was situated in a quiet cul-de-sac and Maya liked it.

The new house looked similar to their previous one and had comparable features. She still had a spacious room to herself, and she loved it. The summer holiday went very quickly and was mainly taken up with packing and unpacking loads of boxes and settling in their new home.

In the September following the summer holidays, Maya decided to take a breath of fresh air and give life another chance; a fresh start at schoolwork, behavior and friendship; and all the other elements that life could hand an eleven-year-old girl.

She made peace with herself, found joy in her life, and appreciated the opportunity to attend a Grammar School. Life opened up in colours for Maya and she soon discovered that whenever she changed the way she looked at things, the things she looked at changed. That was very interesting; the things she looked at didn't change in physical form. Maya was smart enough to know that. What she recognized was more philosophical than physical. Whenever she decided to look at a challenge differently, she soon realized that her outlook on the challenge changed. If she previously thought a task was impossible to solve, as she took a different look, solutions sprang at her. This would have been baffling to any Year Seven student but not Maya. She was curious, and excited; eager to discover more philosophical algorithms for herself.

Maya also willingly made two new friends; Aries and Penelope. Also, in the summer holidays following the completion of Junior School, in addition to their relocating, Maya had attended a two-week summer school for skating. This helped her a lot. She had begun working on her perception of herself and started liking herself more, a necessary ingredient at such a crucial transitional stage in her life.

Maya was a truly fortunate girl. With an increased awareness of the rarity of her social circumstances, she counted herself privileged to be where she was and started being a lot more grateful for the little things she often took for granted. As her self-esteem grew so did her confidence. She was learning to deal with any social problems she encountered, more appreciably and with maturity.

High School was a lot different from Junior School. As Maya discovered in her first year, she had to take responsibility for her routines and timetables and needed to work hard at all her subjects. To do this, she had to come to terms with the fact that her previous behaviours must completely be stamped out. She started trusting her teachers and approaching them for support more than she did in her previous schools. Mrs. Dickson was very supportive of Maya. She registered her for after-school activities that could benefit her social skills. Having previously been a secondary school teacher, Mrs. Dickson was interested in Maya's learning and schoolwork and started tutoring her at home for an hour each day. It wasn't long before everyone noticed that Maya was asking and answering more questions in class, more than anyone else in fact. The teachers noticed her high grades and were quick to commend Maya on her performance. After her end of term exams in Year Eight, she was in the year group's top three percent for all her subjects. Now, that was truly magnanimous! In a school with five forms for each year group and twenty students in each class, being in the top three percent meant that Maya was one of three extremely intelligent and outstanding students in her year. Maya was also identified as an exceptionally talented student. With this revelation, she resolved that she was not going to be an average student anymore. She was going to be her best at everything. As her psychological state improved, Maya realized that the bouts of paralysis she had often experienced completely ceased. She had read that poetry helped keep a calm mind, so she started memorizing lots of different poems. With her eloquence of speech and wealth of words, Maya developed a hunger for writing and a creative style of expression in her writing. Her writings mimicked her own character: expressive and unpredictably innovative. She began exercising a great sense of calmness and strength of mind and with that came a string of writing awards and 'student of the month' nominations from the school's English department. It was therefore no surprise when one of her stories got chosen as the winner of the school's story writing competition. Maya had written the piece merely by an inspiration from her garden and had titled it: 'A Regrettable Wet Woolbeck Blanket'. With shaky hands, Maya stood up in assembly and read her story to the whole school:

A Regrettable Wet Woolbeck Blanket By Maya Dickson

Woolbeck Blanket stood outside in their garden all alone, feeling rather forlorn. The garden, very large and decorated with shrubs and lanky petals was a delightful sight to behold. But even in its gorgeous state, the garden provided no comfort for Woolbeck. He felt lost and alone and he languished in his pitiful thoughts surrounded by dreary and dejected shadows, teasingly dancing to his whimpering. Once warm, dry and cheerful - a necessary comfort in a cozy bed on a cold night- Woolbeck now looked like a rather miserable, glum and abandoned hermit.

Looking through the window, he could see Lucky and Squishy, his siblings, cozily arranged on the couch, enjoying a splash ambience of tranquility and enviable giggles. A great cloud of anxiety washed over Woolbeck as his thoughts drifted onto what looked like a night in the drizzles and dew, with occasional drops of unwanted waste material from partying flyers whose empathy for the homeless had long departed their souls. These flying birds were rather thoughtless at the most unimaginable times. Indeed, they flew about with no care in the world, no, not a thought for whoever needed it.

The living room curtains pulled together and soon the night was near for the Redwop-Shaw-Blanket household. Presently, the dimmed light became a thing of the past. The garden was soon translated into a 16th century dark hole with no hope of life whatsoever. Woolbeck looked to his left and to his right. He was sore scared and confused, as confused as a rabbit in headlights. The neighbourhood felt silent; a deeply-piercing silence. a silence too loud for comfort. Everyone seemed to have gone on a deeply disturbing long journey into Dreamland. Even the streetlights were stingingly dim, with barely any flicker of hope. "Can grown-up boys feel fear?" Woolbeck whispered to himself. He has always been the brave, bold and daring one in the Blanket family. He had often ventured with his body where others' minds trembled to float.

Woolbeck closed his eyes and took a deep breath, preparing his once tenacious body, now limb and lacking strength, for another opportunity to receive sunshine into his mind. Sunshine and heat bring life to his soul; it is these which revive him and give him hope to prepare for wet days. Finally, he exhaled, mind poised to take on the night and as if on cue, the sky unleashed its fury. Anger roared and thunder clapped. The heavens screamed with

*accolades, behold the mighty waters were
descending strings of stairs. Who dared stood in
their way? It poured and whipped; Woolbeck was
drenched and soaked. When it was all over, he
stood completely unrecognisable and truly
unattractive; a shadow of his old self, bedraggled
and broken in spirit. Who will be drawn to a wet
Blanket? He was too weak to fight back. Ridiculous
as he looked, he admitted that for once, he had
acted foolishly. Sometimes it's better to be looked
on as a coward than to try being valiant and die a
fool. All he needed right now, was just a tender
squeeze to ease off his wretchedness; to desperately
cure that tinge of ache on his wrists, shoulders and
waist and clear the accumulation of fluid in his legs
that is so needing a cure. Continuous needless
exposure to cold water brings on arthritis, he's
been told. Must he suffer arthritis at this tender
age? Woolbeck Redwop- Shaw-Blanket's vivacious
reflections soon transcended his gloom and
canopied his tears. His vivid considerations drifted
into placid catnap and soon he was asleep, snoring
and dreaming of the pulsating sunshine that often
whistled to him from his bedroom window. He
dreamed and smiled and hugged his body with his
warm covers. Then Woolbeck awoke with a start!
What on earth is it that is applying a pulling force
to his delicate skin? The neighbour's cat continued*

*his play, undisturbed by the fact that he was
actually intruding into Woolbeck's delicate state.
With one last wrench, the cat managed to snatch its
nap away and with that, Woolbeck shot to complete
wakefulness.*

*He let out a loud scream, a shrill screech, then
another scream before breaking into a joyful tune.
Mrs Redwop-Shaw-Blanket tenderly took him off the
drying line and with a mighty twist, wrung the last
of the fluid out of him, gave him an active flap over
her knees and folded him over her shoulders. "Why
hadn't anyone noticed my long absence?"
Woolbeck asked furiously. "Didn't anyone miss me
at all?" he continued. "Is there no one whose
existence absolutely depended on me enough to
have run a team in search for me?" Woolbeck
continued with his tirade of questioning. Inside the
house, he was introduced to a warm press and soon
was snuggled in the couch, folded in three areas,
just as he liked it.*

*Never again will Woolbeck Blanket seek such a
mindless and dangerous adventure. There are safer
pranks to play besides toppling out of bedroom
windowsills. He had always wondered what it felt
like to glide down those sloppy roof tops. What he
hadn't realised was that he risked being locked out
of the house and left at the mercy of chastising*

weather.

Woolbeck Blanket had learnt a big lesson. Next time, he was sure to remember to keep his patty feet where they're meant to be and his wild thoughts on the check.

After all, nobody likes a wet Blanket!

The End

Maya's story deserved the attention it got; it was unbelievably ingenious. Even she had to constantly pinch herself to reality. "Who would have thought that she had such inspired story threads in her?" she asked rhetorically.

Yes, Maya had found yet another connection to reach her world. This was a most phenomenal awakening.

Her skating got some more attention in High School too. South Wilts Grammar School encouraged students involvement in diverse sporting activities so Maya had the opportunity to pursue some swimming as well as tennis, in addition to her skating.

Despite these other interests, she kept her passion for skating, attending an after-school skating club every Tuesday evening, and Sunday afternoon throughout the winter term. This meant that she missed out on a few social activities with Aries and Penelope. She also missed out on some parties with the rest of her class girls, but she didn't mind. By this time in her life, Maya was beginning to realize that she couldn't have everything, so she needed to make important choices. If she wanted to keep excelling in her academic work and her skating at the same time, then she ought to prioritise and make some sacrifices.

In the spring of Year Ten, South Wilts Grammar School entered a number of students in a national teen skating competition. Maya was fortunate to be one of them. Together there were six students. With a focused mind and a determined attitude, Maya started practicing for an hour after school each day and she worked as if her life depended on it. Maya routinely went to the park with Mrs. Dickson where it was spacious and quiet, to make use of the skating platform. To add to that, on Saturdays, she went to the recreational centre with Mr. Dickson, where she had a three-hour one-to-one skating coaching. Maya was having a wonderful time. She barely looked or sounded like the old Margarine. She loved every minute she spent skating and soon she had over-mastered her choreography. She worked on her free-style too but took care to not injure herself as this involved jumps, spins and choreographed movements to music.

Occasionally, Maya would remember her challenging childhood and the fact that she was still quite a sensitive person. She often asked about her mother and her Godparents were always willing to answer any questions on her mind. She had never met her dad who supposedly was back in prison for other grave offences. Her mum had lived in a flat in some part of London, where she and Mrs. Dickson visited once, but that was a few years ago. She didn't particularly warm up to the state of the flat. They had to navigate dozens of steps which had scribbling of inappropriate words and drawings everywhere. Maya recalled the stench she had to boldly endure and the torture of hopping stairs to steer clear of vomit lavishly spewed about. The state of the flat itself was a total embarrassment to humanity. Oozing with foul smell, one could taste the air without even trying. When her mum greeted them at the front door, she looked like something the cat had dragged in, out of desperation. Maya was sad at the thought that her mum hadn't bothered at a better presentation. Obviously, the whole estate needed extensive sorting but her mum could have attended to her flat and her body with some thought. Mrs. Dickson and Maya barely said hello and were out of the flat like a spot of rash. Maya was disgusted; hugely traumatised. That was the first meeting she had had with her mum since her adoption at age seven, having been separated from her and taken into care at a tender age.

Older now, Maya was aware that her mum had a new flat; was cleaner and healthier but was also aware that her mum had been in and out of drug and alcohol rehabilitation centres to get her life sorted and even though she was no longer Maya's legal guardian, they were free to see each other occasionally at Maya's discretion. Maya remained hesitant.

During one Easter holiday, however, Maya and her Godparents agreed that she could spend a weekend with Variella at her new flat. Maya was a responsible teenager and very capable of looking after herself. She had shown a high level of care and responsibility and could be completely trusted to spend some private time with her mum. Mrs. Dickson took Maya to the train station from where her mum picked her up. She was happy to see her mother, though slightly unsure of her. She behaved very politely, and the afternoon went on rather well, without any alarm. Maya needed to either embrace her mum's position in her life or bring closure to any existing connection between them. Meeting her was therefore of great significance to their delicate and somehow derailed relationship.

They strolled in the town, and Maya even braved up to holding her mum's hand. They did some window shopping and went into an ice-cream parlour for a snack. Conversation between the two was obviously awkward, but being a well-mannered young lady, Maya made small talk and appeared interested in her mum's 'not-so-sordid' life.

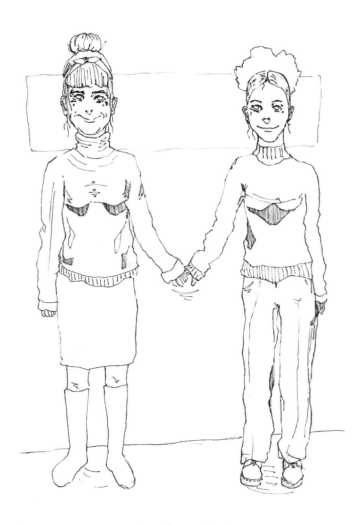

As it was a sunny day, they joined an 'open top' bus for a ride into London to see a carnival.

Maya had fun watching the carnival procession, after which they went into a local pub for some mouth-watering fish and chips with mushy peas. Her mum excused herself and went to use the toilet. She returned looking rather strangely dazed. In the middle of lunch her mum needed to use the toilet three more times and each time she came out looking even more strange. Maya started hearing alarm bells, but she did not panic. Thirty minutes later, her mum could barely stand on her feet. Her words were blurry and hard to understand. Maya walked to the manager at the bar and explained her mother's situation; the police were called in and so was an ambulance. Maya never got to spend the weekend at her mum's flat and as she watched her mum being carried away into the ambulance, she knew that they might not meet again. Her mum was still not fit to be with. Mrs. Dickson was quickly notified of the developments and after over a two-hour wait at the police station, Maya was picked up by her Godmother. A police lady had sat with her for most of the time and had calmly explained her mum's state. If Maya hadn't been so upset, she might actually have joked about her biological name - Cops- but with disappointment seething through her skin, she was too emotional to express any humour. She was very quiet during the long journey back home but was determined not to slope backward. A few days later at home, when she was ready to speak about the incident, Mr. and Mrs.

Dickson were kind and understanding, and offered her a sound platform to air all grievances. Maya handled the situation very maturely. In her heart, she knew that it was time to accept that she was not going to have a meaningful relationship with her biological mum or dad. It was time she completely saw Mr. and Mrs. Dickson as her true parents. After all, she was Maya Dickson, not Margarine Cops. Once she had reached this decision, she became calm.

It was musical calling the Dicksons 'mum' and 'dad' and even though it was slightly strange, the new experience was also totally titillating for Maya who used every opportunity to say the two words.

School life was fantastic. Maya was getting better and better each day. She focused on her schoolwork and utilised her newly gained confidence. She made sure that schoolwork and skating both received enough attention so she could be at her best. By now, it was five weeks to the national teen skating competition. Maya was confident that she had done enough work on her routines and techniques to grant her a top position in the finals. She had no doubt that she would sail through the preliminary stages.

Each day she practiced and each time she got better

and learnt something new. Maya loved quotes; just like poems, they kept her passion alive for her pursuits. Maya mused on a quote and thoughtfully entrenching it in her heart, she reflected on it: "the most important thing about skating is that it teaches you to do the things you should do before you do the things you want to do." She repeatedly recited the quote as if to make a point to herself. In actual fact, skating is a discipline that had and continued to thoroughly shape her attitude to and management of her life. Through that, she had learnt to set goals and to block out distractions and all other things and to just focus, focus only on one thing at a time. Maya looked after herself and followed a healthy diet as well as balanced sleep pattern to keep a fresh state.

The long-anticipated day soon arrived. Maya and the other five competitors from her school were accompanied by their Headteacher, P.E teacher and another member of staff. There were fifteen high schools competing altogether and in total they produced ninety students. The competition took place in a very large roofed outdoor arena which was part of a gymnasium, a phenomenally big environment with intimidating features.

Each of the competitors was allocated a cubicle to get changed in and lockers to keep their belongings.

They each had a name tag and a school badge to stick on their show outfits. Maya wore gold skating tights and a sparkling gold long-sleeved leotard. She had a short, red, wrap skirt around her waist and also wore protective pads over her knees and elbows. Finally, she put on her identification tag and wore her skating shoes.

Maya was ready to face the crowd. She glided with the rest of the skating squad onto the arena to make their entrance curtsy. She felt very proud of herself and knew that Mrs. Dickson, her caring mum, was watching from one of the stands and wishing her well. She also knew that her dad, Mr. Dickson was also there with a big yellow handkerchief, waving energetically from the crowd. Different thoughts started running through her mind and soon she broke into a sweat. She took one glance towards where she knew her mum would be sitting and her voice echoed in her head almost instantly "You are the best, Maya. This is your dream and if you put your mind to it, you can make it a reality. Remember, your energy flows where your attention goes, so control your focus." Maya had envisaged and relished the approach of this day and was now more than ever, certain that she had made the right choice. She desired nothing more at that minute and would never have changed any part of her life at that point, including her choice of sports. Dance skating was her outlet, an opening for her, the very essence of her life; it was her breath, it was how she had transcended her many childhood problems and lived. Dance skating allowed her to transmit every emotion she felt and gave her hope for life. Yes, dance skating really drew appreciation from her and made every pain and every sacrifice she had gone through well worth it.

Maya heard her name, so she straightened up and curtsied to the crowd. This was her first national competition and she wanted to win it. At this stage, winning carried a certain significance. It was not the fact of beating an opponent or performing above all else. It was a sign that she had changed, that she was learning and that she was excelling in her learning. So, Maya wanted to win. Winning there in that huge arena, in front of all the people she cared about was not a 'sometime' thing; it was a 'nowtime' thing which she had developed the frequency for, all the time. Maya was now a student of life who knew that one didn't win occasionally; one didn't do the right things only once in a while. No, in life, you do right all the time. Maya's journey had been long, unsteady, and often convoluted in some parts, but in all its meanderings, her journey had taught her that winning was a habit that needed to be cultivated and entrenched.

Yes, Maya Dickson wasn't in the competition just to have fun and leave with a consolation prize. She was there to build memories, record an experience of a lifetime, have fun, and then win! She also knew that there were eighty-nine other competitors who had their eyes on that same title and trophy.

With the thousand thoughts floating in her mind, Maya finished her curtsy, looked up, smiled and waved. Then she took to the floor. Maya let her energies out and intensely immersed in her performance. When she was done, her head felt light and her feet could barely hold on to the floor. Gingerly, she curtsied and made her way to her changing room to freshen up, change outfits and get ready for her next round.

After three hours of fierce competition, the number
of competitors narrowed down to twenty.

Another round of competing and there were only

ten competitors left. Maya was still in it. There was an hour break before the quarter finals. After a further one-hour session, there were five students through to the semi-finals. The competition had become very tough, and tiredness had set in but Maya was determined to keep her focus. She valued the need to rule her own mind, and treasured the significance of the notion that conquering her mind and bringing her focus under complete control would be her greatest act. It was also that which could ultimately grant her the victory she so greatly desired.

After the break and the semi-final session, only three contestants proceeded into the finals; with Maya being the only competitor from her school. Maya knew that each of the three of them was guaranteed a prize, however she was not in the competition to win just any prize. She wanted the first prize, championship title, and the gold trophy. Her mind was made up. She had faith, she was disciplined, and she had been a consistent and selfless devotee to her skating, now the heavens were her limit, not the sky.

In the final event, each of the three competitors had to do a display of their own unique compositions and techniques. Maya knew from experiences in local competitions that the judges were looking out for originality, confidence, and charm in the individual compositions. However, they were also looking for accuracy of steps when performing particular dance routines. In addition to this, she had to be accurate on her edges and turns and particularly as a dance skater, she must carry herself in an elegant manner while paying careful attention to the rhythm and timing of the music. Yes, Maya knew that it was time for her to be positively Flappity Maya.

Her thoughts were jumbled as she contemplated how to introduce all the different routines in a timely and orderly fashion. Maya took in a deep breath of fresh air, organised her mind with a recital of one of her favourite and most cherished poems; then decided that it was truly now or never. She watched as each of the other two girls took to the platform and enchanted the judges with their various styles. Soon she heard her name and took her curtsy.

She glided to the centre of the platform and entered into her haven. She was completely unaware of her surroundings as she performed a show-stopper. Her glides and turns were beyond belief and the applause that followed each movement was deafening. The whole venue was alive with people screaming and clapping endlessly. Everyone was on their feet. Maya knew she had done her best, particularly when she spotted her dad's big yellow butterfly handkerchief waving madly in the air. She wanted to win the show but more significantly, she knew that her life was changed forever.

5

Be a champion or be consoled

Maya stood on the impeccable winner's podium holding a bouquet of flowers, her glittery gold trophy and £2000 cheque reward safely placed on the trophy stand. She requested to say a few words. First, she congratulated the eighty-nine competitors who had started with her and offered

commiserations to the two finalists who won second and third places. She then expressed gratitude to all the people whose various sensible choices and actions had preserved her life. Maya knew that her life could have been a different story altogether, probably one that wouldn't have made even an owl blink! She thought of the many dangerous things she had exposed herself to as a child.

"So you see, my life could have been destroyed from consuming that huge amount of paracetamol syrup. I could have incurred permanent damage to my limbs from that reckless jump when I was a little girl, if the gardener hadn't looked up at that very moment." There was complete silence in the gymnasium. Every ear was listening to Maya. "I was once a Margarine issue, a child who left a lot of distaste wherever she went." She looked at her bouquet, as if for inspiration. "Looking back, I recognise that my life was a gift, now I know. Suddenly, I understand why a wonderful couple who had a great life, wanted me, a bundle of hazard, in their lives; it was all part of the gift." Maya paused. There wasn't a single 'dry eye' in the gymnasium. It looked as though everyone was shedding a 'Maya tear'. Maya thanked her parents, Mr. and Mrs. Dickson, for rescuing her from the Cops, believing in her and willingly investing a myriad of resources in her. She thanked the competition organisers, the various sponsors, and again, acknowledged the other competitors from the different schools. Then she thanked her Headteacher, schoolteachers, club trainer and her school mates and fellow competitors again, for their support. Completely overwhelmed with emotions she paused and briefly reflected on her life. With trembling voice, she ended her speech with the following words: "It does not matter to me anymore that growing up, I didn't have regular parents or that I was adopted as a young child. What matters is that I found the positive end of life early enough and I held on to it. I changed my inner persuasions, redirected my focus and that has changed my life forever."

There was a loud round of applause as everyone stood on their feet once more. Maya's parents, Head teacher, club trainer, teachers and school mates gathered around her happily. Without any inhibitions, she hugged her parents tightly and sobbed with joy. Finally, she lifted the trophy as high as she could and gave out a loud ear-splitting scream, the kind only Maya could do: "Yeeeessss, Flappity Maya did it!" "Of course, Flappity, you did what only you could do." Her mum's voice sounded softly. "Well done, my dear," added Mrs. Dickson, "and for that we got you a wrapped freckled present." She finished off with a cheeky smile.

After ceremonial photos had been taken and enough congratulations and commiserations offered, Mr. and Mrs. Dickson led Maya out of the gymnasium into the arena restaurant. A man in black trousers and navy blazer stood next to a woman in beige tailored suit; they both had their backs to the door. A teenage looking boy, wearing a maroon long sleeved shirt with black trousers and holding what looked like a journal, stood to the right of the woman and was engrossed in a conversation with her.

Maya blinked when the boy turned. "No, it can't be, it can't be!" "Carwyn! Carwyn Driscoll?" She was shocked. "Freckled Carwyn, my friend?" Maya screamed. "Oh, my word, it's Carwyn!" The grown-ups looked at one another and laughed.

A stroll down memory lane

Carwyn: Hello Maya, I'm glad to see you again. It's been a very long time. You look the same but somehow in a different way.

Maya: I could say the same about you. You've become very tall. I'm happy to see you too. How are you and where have you been?

Carwyn: It's a very long story but first congratulations on your performance and winning. You did a fantastic job out there. (reached to a nearby table and produced a beautiful bouquet of flowers).

Maya: Thank you … wait, how do you know I did a fantastic job out there? Were you watching?

Carwyn: *Silence*

Maya: (Getting very comfortable and falling into an old habit, lightly kicked him on his shin). You were watching? How did you know I was performing? How did you even know where I was? *Turns to parents who avoid her gaze.*

Carwyn: After our accident and subsequent discharge from the hospital, we stayed in Wales so I could attend physiotherapy and rehabilitation for my walking. I was admitted to a new school. On completing Year Six, I gained admission to a good secondary school which I attended for two years. We missed England so my parents arranged a visit, with the possibility of relocating. During our time away, we rented out our old house, so the plan was to move back in. We arrived back in England with great expectations only to discover that you had moved. There were new people in your old house. The lovely next-door neighbours who lived to the right of your house had apparently joined their daughter in New Zealand. No one had contacts for you. We even went to our old school, but they had a new Head teacher who didn't know us and couldn't help at all, something to do with data protection. The neighbourhood seemed very different as though in the three years every familiar face had been transported away somewhere. My parents had difficulty settling in as well so when my dad got a job with a law firm in a town called Devizes in Wiltshire, we moved.

I started a new secondary school and my mum got a job in a nearby girls' grammar school. Mum had to stay in school for a late students' progress and parents' consultation meeting one day and as my dad and I were waiting in the car park to pick her up, we saw a man and a lady, walking into the school with a teenage girl. It was nothing unusual except for when right across the car park, another girl shouted the name 'Maya' and ran up to meet them. It was at this time that my dad sat up in the car, eyes wide with surprise. We realised instantly that it was you with Mr. and Mrs. Dickson. In the weeks that followed, having realised you attended the girls' school where my mum taught, we determined to investigate if that was truly you. My mum knew by our ages what school year group you'll be in so she spoke with all the form tutors and it turned out that it was most definitely you. My parents quickly got in touch with yours and they have been meeting for coffee and catching up for a month now. They had to keep it from you so that you could focus on your competition. Afterwards, the obvious plan was to present me as a present. I dreaded the idea of this whole secret, but I had to go along.

Maya: (speechless for about a minute). If your mum is a teacher in my school, how is it that I did not realise a link with the name? This is totally beyond belief. It's really you Carwyn Driscoll, I'm glad you're alive! Goodness, you've had such a growth spurt. If I hadn't seen your freckles and that conspicuous birth mark on your ear, I probably would not have made you out.

Carwyn: Yes, Maya. It's the same freckled me! You

know that my name is of Welsh origin, right?

Maya: Right!

Carwyn: Well, it's not just a name you know, it's a name with deep meaning: 'loved and blessed'.

Maya: Oh Carwyn, I see that you still have your sense of humour. Next thing I know is you'll be telling me your granddad invented 'rock, paper, scissors'.

Carwyn: Yes, I still do have my sense of humour Maya, but my name does mean 'loved and blessed', how else do you think I survived my injuries from the accident? He added with a cheeky smile. My parents were not as badly injured as I was. They didn't think I was going to make it with my limbs intact. That's all in the past now. See, I brought back the journal you gave me and I used a gel pen as you instructed and wrote every detail of my holidays in it. After my recovery from the accident, I kept writing. I was sure that I was going to meet you somewhere someday. I'm glad I kept it.

Maya: (with tears in her eyes) Thank you Carwyn, I'm glad you're here, and fully recovered. You're truly my best friend.

Mirror image

Mrs. Nibbs stopped reading. She looked from one child to the other and smiled. The children had all been sitting on the grass quietly, engrossed in listening to her for a rather long time. The story was so captivating that none of them had interrupted, not even Ralph. There had been no "please Miss, may I go to the toilet" or "please Miss, I need a drink of water." Mrs. Nibbs was very impressed indeed. "That was a successful afternoon," she commented. "Yes, Miss, we even got Christopher F and Christopher M sitting next to each other and they are still in two full bodies, no clawing at each other!" added Celine in her tiny voice. Everyone giggled in agreement.

"Do you know what, children?" Mrs. Nibbs broke the silence. "Maya and Carwyn remained very good friends even though at this stage they each had their circle of other friends. Maya continued excelling in her skating and in her schoolwork and later obtained a scholarship to study English and Drama at Oxford University.

As for Carwyn, his interest in cycling brought him into contact with many sport personalities out of which he earned a two-year internship to Denmark with a major sports club as a trainee physiotherapist. On his return, he went off to study Sports Psychology at Loughborough University."

The children still sat quietly, no one showed signs of moving. They were inextricably wound into the story so much that they didn't realise to question Mrs. Nibbs about the last statements she had made about Maya and Carwyn; how she came to know that detail of their lives. As no one interrupted, Mrs. Nibbs continued her talking: "Just like Maya's character, life can have some very tricky twists to it. When things seem very bad, all we need is to believe that we'll go to sleep at night and have a fresh start the next day. Sometimes even with a new and fresh day, the problems often remain but we still need to be cheerful and optimistic. It's a bit like when it's sunny and you want to go out and play then suddenly it starts raining. You know what I often encourage you to do during those times?" "Yes, Mrs. Nibbs," the class chanted, "to line up at the window and look up the sky for that glorious and fluorescent rainbow."

The children of Year 6 Goldilocks class were as quiet as church mice, so quiet the susurration of the leaves on the trees were audible. In a most surreal manner, Mrs. Nibbs led all the children back into class. Once settled in their seats, she opened her private teacher's cupboard and brought out a beautifully framed picture of a curly-haired teenaged child proudly holding a trophy. At first nobody understood nor did the link click. Then Yemuel stood from the back of the class, gingerly walked towards Mrs. Nibbs and peered into her face, gently touching her hair. Then he took the framed picture and looked at the teenage girl's face. All was silent. The children seemed to have clocked the secret.

The notoriously noisy Year 6 Goldilocks class went speechless. The class, for once, held a record-breaking silence for two minutes. They were as silent as a cemetery and when the hush lifted, the murmuring was still as quiet as church mice. Then one after the other, they started clapping. It was like the sound of thunder. Then without warning, Yemuel gave his teacher a big hug. One by one, the whole class raced to the front and flung their arms around their teacher. The school bell had rung for home time, but Year 6 Goldilocks hadn't heard it at all. By now the class door was lined up with confused and bemused parents, eagerly waiting for their children but certainly observing the interesting happenings in the classroom.

Ten minutes later, when all was back to normal, the class door opened with each child looking as though they had had a watershed moment on a wonderful adventure. As if a spell had been cast over them, each child kept a smile on their face even long after they had departed from the school gates.

The weeks that followed were never the same. Nobody dared ask what had transpired in the Year 6 Goldilocks class, because what ever took place on that fateful afternoon, had transformed the children beyond recognition, and the whole school preferred to let sleeping dogs lie, or else the notorious Year 6 Goldilocks might resurrect.

The End!

DISCUSSION POINTS AFTER READING

With your child, see if you can play a game and come up with meanings to the following phrases and idiomatic expressions as used in the book. You can look up the meanings of these phrases and expressions below:

1.   "Enthusiasm written all over their faces"

2.   "Put a lid on it"

3.   "Deaf ears"

4.   "Jump through hoops"

5.   "Frazzled by her frenzies"

6.   "Let sleeping dogs lie"

7.   "Rumbling on like a pot of boiling potatoes"

8.   "Over the moon"

9.   "At the speed of lightning"

10.   "As quiet as church mice"

11.   "Beggars can't be choosers "

12.   "Silver spoon"

13.   "As fortune would have it"

Meanings to Discussion Points

Here are some meanings to the phrases and idiomatic expressions used in the book.

1. "Enthusiasm written all over their faces" – Looking cheerful and expecting something good.

2. "Put a lid on it" – Keep one's voice down/ keep quiet.

3. "Deaf ears" – Closed ears/ not listening.

4. "Jump through hoops" – Do just about anything possible.

5. "Frazzled by her frenzies" – Disturbed by someone's agitations.

6. "Let sleeping dogs lie" - Allow peace to be.

7. "Rumbling on like a pot of boiling potatoes" – Over-talking and making no sense.

8. "Over the moon"- Overjoyed.

9. "At the speed of lightning" – Quicker than could be imagined.

10. "As quiet as church mice" – Not making a sound.

11. " Beggars can't be choosers" – You have no option so you take what you're given.

12. " Silver spoon" – Riches or inheritance.

13. "As fortune would have it" – Success, blessing or goodwill that was not planned and was unexpected.

Maya Poems

1. The Champion Skater – A Kenning poem

2. Grass To Grace – A Rhyming poem

From Author To Reader:

In life, children are born into unique domestic circumstances entirely outside of their control. Regardless of how, where and with whom you spend your childhood, your future doesn't have to be compromised.

Human beings can rise above very tough situations and overcome almost any challenge.

Did You Know?

1. Melissa Gilbert, an American actor who featured in 'Little House on the Prairie', was adopted soon after birth by Paul Gilbert.
2. Nicole Richie, American fashion designer, singer and T.V personality, was raised by Lionel Richie and his wife at the time (Brenda), at the age of three and subsequently adopted when she was 9 years.
3. Debbie Harry, lead singer and front woman of iconic band Blondie, was adopted at just three months old.
4. The late Steve Jobs was an American pioneer in personal computers who was given up and adopted at birth.

5. Nicky Campbell, a British journalist, TV and radio presenter, was adopted by Scottish couple Frank and Sheila Campbell just days after he was born.

6. The late Nelson Mandela was South Africa's first black chief executive and the first president elected in a fully representative democratic election. After his father's death, Nelson Mandela was adopted at the age of nine by Chief Jongintaba Dalindyebo, the acting regent of the Thembu people.

7. Eddie Murphy, an iconic American comedian, actor, writer, singer and director was temporarily placed in foster care, together with his brother, at a time when his family was struggling financially.

8. Cher, an American singer, actress, entertainer, and fashion icon, was very young when her mother and father separated making life very difficult. Her mother was forced to put her into foster care as she couldn't financially support her.

9. Toby Anstis, a British radio presenter, was adopted, alongside his twin sister Kate, when he was just six weeks old.

10. The late John Lennon was abandoned by his father when he was 3years and his mum

decided she could no longer look after him. He was taken up and raised by his aunt.

11. Eric Clapton, an English rock and blues guitarist, singer and songwriter, grew up believing his grandparents were his parents and that his mother who was16 when he was born, was his sister.

12. Michael Oher, an American footballer was adopted at the age of 17 after he had spent several years in foster homes.

13. Bill Clinton, the 42nd U.S president, was looked after by paternal grandparents from birth and later adopted by his stepfather.

14. Les Brown is an American motivational speaker, former Ohio politician, popular author and radio DJ. He was born in an abandoned building and given up for adoption. He was later adopted by Mamie Brown, a 38-year-old single woman who worked as a cafeteria attendant and domestic assistant.

15. The late Marilyn Monroe was a famous American actor, singer and model who was abandoned by her widowed mum and so she spent most of her childhood in foster homes.

GLOSSARY

Ability: Power to do something.

Accompany: Go along with.

Accuracy: Correctness.

Acknowledge: Admit or accept.

Accolades: Public recognition.

Adherence: The power to stick to something.

Adjustment: Becoming used to new situations.

Anticipate: Expect or predict something.

Applause: Show approval or praise.

Aquarium: A place where live fish and other water creatures and plants are kept.

Assimilate: To learn or to be part of.

Astute: Smart.

Avert: Prevent.

Barely: Only just/almost not.

Belabour: Overdo.

Bestow: Bless with.

Biological: Natural/real/actual.

Blurry: Cannot be heard clearly.

Bulging: Sticking out or protruding.

Charm: Power to delight or attract others.

Choreography: The order of steps or movements in staged dance.

Clumping: A heavy dull sound like a thud.

Commend: To praise.

Composition: The action of putting things together.

Confidence: The feeling that one can rely on someone or something.

Consolation: Comfort after a disappointment.

Critical: Dangerous/very important stage.

Cubicle: A small, separated area of a room.

Cul-de-sac: A street or passage closed at one end.

Determined: To decide firmly.

Discretion: The freedom to decide what should be done in a particular situation.

Display: Performance, show or event.

Disruptive: Interrupt by causing a problem or disturbance.

Echo: Sound repeated.

Ecstatic: Extremely joyful.

Elegant: Pleasingly graceful in appearance.

Enchant: To fill someone with great delight.

Endear: Make appealing.

Fierce: Having or displaying intense aggressiveness.

Flair: Skill, ability or talent.

Flared: Spread.

Focus: The act of concentrating interest.

Frazzled: Tired out.

Frenetic: Chaotic.

Frenzy: Wild excitement.

Gabbling: Talking rapidly and unintelligibly.

Ginormous: Extremely large.

Glide: Move with smooth continuous motion.

Guardian: A person who looks after and is legally responsible for someone.

Gymnasium: A room or building equipped for gymnastics, games and other physical exercise.

Higgledy-piggledy: Untidy, messy and disorganised.

Idleness: Avoidance of work, laziness.

Incapable: Unable to do something.

Invigorate: Energise.

Jolt: Shock or shake.

Jumble: An untidy collection.

Leotard: Close fitting one-piece garment made from stretchy fabric covering a person's body from shoulder to top of the thighs typically worn by dancers, gymnasts and people exercising indoors.

Manner: A way in which a thing is done.

Mount: Climb up or move up on to a raised surface.

Myriad: Countless or extremely great number.

Nonentity: A person with no special qualities; an unimportant person.

Notify: Inform someone of something.

Notorious: Not respectable or respectful.

Oblivious: Unaware of.

Obnoxious: Unpleasant and annoying.

Orderly: Neatly arranged.

Originality: Quality of being new or unusual.

Overwhelm: Overcome or amaze.

Perception: View or opinion.

Plummet: Drop in size.

Preliminary: An action done in preparation for something higher or more important.

Prioritise: Determine the order for dealing with items or tasks.

Refrain: Hold back, stop oneself or withhold from doing something.

Rehabilitation: The act of restoring to normal health or life.

Relocate: Move to a new place and making one's home there.

Reputation: Opinions held about someone or something.

Resolve: Settle or find a solution to some problem.

Routine: Sequence of actions regularly followed.

Rhythm: Regular repeated pattern of movement or sound.

Saddle: To burden.

Significant: Important and worthy of attention.

Slump: To sink, slouch or fall heavily.

Soliloquize: Talk to oneself.

Spectacular: Impressive to look at.

Splay: To spread out and apart.

Succulent: Exciting and interesting or pleasant to the taste.

Susurration: Whispering or rustling

Technique: Detail and method of doing something.

Tempestuous: Filled with a state of emotional instability.

Thrill: Fill with excitement and pleasure.

Throbbing: Regular rhythmic beat.

Toddle: Walking with short unsteady steps.

Tortuous: Of a twisty and difficult nature.

Tremendous: Very great in amount or intensity.

Trudge: Walk with slow heavy steps.

Undeterred: Not put off.

Undisputed: Unquestionable.

Unique: Being the only one of its kind.

Utilise: Make practical and effective use of something.

Unperturbed: Calm, without signs of worry.

Volatile: Having a tendency to break out.

Yearning: A strong desire.

Yelp: Short sharp high pitched barking.

HELP YOUR CHILD READ

The 'Issue' of Flappity Maya is a story aimed at supporting, motivating and encouraging pleasurable reading in children.

It captures aspects of life represented in different social and family situations; particularly for children who grew up in foster care or were adopted. The story employs a combination of carefully chosen simple and ambitious vocabulary and fictional language to foster enjoyment and good comprehension of the genre.

Additionally, it uses common daily activities and experiences to create simple understanding of the various generic ways in which certain children experience childhood.

In reading this book children will come to reinforce the recognition that fundamentally human beings are the same. However, various social, family and upbringing experiences introduce uniqueness to each individual. This, in itself, can aid their appreciation of positive diversity in the world.

The 'Issue' of Flappity Maya uses very simple toned-down and illustrations to generate fun and creative thinking.

115

Read regularly with your child and create opportunities for independent reading as well. Reading helps build confidence and a sense of efficacy in children and can be a source of fun.

As you go over the pages, look at the pictures and talk about what you see.

May be take the opportunity to re-read the story of *'A Regrettable Wet Woolbeck Blanket By Maya Dickson'*

How would you interpret this story? What were the characters denoting?

I am confident that your child will learn a new word as they read this book. Remember, you can encourage your child to look up unfamiliar words in the glossary at the back of the book.

ABOUT THE AUTHOR

Elizabeth N. Adonu is an educationist with a background in Nursing with Psychology (BA) and Health & Safety Management (MSc). She is also a qualified teacher with a Postgraduate Certificate in Education (PGCE) and currently teaches in a School in the Northamptonshire county, England.

She has worked with various Bedfordshire and Buckinghamshire libraries to support and promote children's reading. In 2011, she launched 'The Smart Reading Child Project' to serve as a support platform for all her engagements and projects. Elizabeth extended her investment in children's education to include story writing and in 2012, published her first children's book: 'The Chase Through Mrs. Remraf's Kitchen'.

Her stories are written with a blend of culture and poetry to stimulate reading enthusiasm and independent reading skills in young readers. She believes that reading helps children expand their minds and nurture creative thinking. This includes motivating children to practice word recital, a venture that can uniquely be deployed through poetry.

OTHER BOOKS BY THE AUTHOR

1. The Chase Through Mrs. Remraf's Kitchen

2. A Taste of Three Continents

Printed in Great Britain
by Amazon